STRIPE THE CLOUD
AND
LIZZIE THE LAMB

Written by Ann Ferry
Illustrated by David Baker

America Star Books

Softcover 9781627724043
PUBLISHED BY AMERICA STAR BOOKS, LLLP
www.americastarbooks.com

Printed in the United States of America

This book is dedicated to my sister Rosemary

Once upon a time, in a land far away, there was a special forest. It was called Featherwood Forest. Many animals lived in Featherweed Forest and all who lived there were very happy. Among the animals who lived in Featherwood Forest was Bristle the Porcupine, who was once a very shy little porcupine, but he had learned to play with all the other animals in the forest and he was now very happy. There was Crackle the Crow, who every day, flew through the forest very early in the morning so that he could have a very tasty breakfast. Spindle the Spider, was a very busy and happy spider who was content to weave and spin her webs all through the forest. Ripples the Frog enjoyed his friends near the pond in the middle of Featherwood Forest.

On the highest tree of the forest, Witty the Owl looked into the forest very often during the day and night. He was very wise. He knew things that the other animals did not know because of his perch on the highest tree in the forest. From there, on the highest perch, he saw things that the other animals in the forest could not see and heard things that the other animals in the forest could not hear.

Close to Featherwood Forest, lay the Village of Ticklefield. The Village of Ticklefield was built in a valley. On both sides of the valley, the mountains spread high and almost touched the clouds. It was springtime now, and on one of the fields in the meadow beyond the Village of Ticklefield, many sheep and lambs wandered. The field was surrounded by thick gorse. The thick gorse and the big gate at the bottom of the field kept the sheep and the lambs safe. There was plenty of green grass for all to eat in the field, in the meadow, high above the Village of Ticklefield.

Meanwhile, up in the sky above Featherwood Forest, the little Clouds were already in the Rainbow Arches Nursery School and almost finished for the day. Today the little Clouds were being dismissed early because their teacher, Mrs. Cloudburst had to meet with Rumbles the Thunder. The class had many little Clouds. There was Gusty the Cloud, Puffy the Cloud, Smudge the Cloud, Racer the Cloud, Patch the Cloud, Shadow the Cloud, Windy the Cloud, Bounce the Cloud, Dollop the Cloud and many other little Clouds who went to school there every day. A new little Cloud who had the happiest smile that Mrs. Cloudburst had ever seen, had started the Rainbow Arches Nursery School today. Her name was Cloud 9. Mrs. Cloudburst knew that there was something very special about her new student.

Mrs. Cloudburst was the only teacher in the Rainbow Arches Nursery School. Mrs. Cloudburst had a lot of energy, and she expected all the little Clouds to listen carefully to her so that they could learn. It was very important to Mrs. Cloudburst that each little Cloud be able to follow her directions, and did everything she asked them to do. To be able to follow directions, the little Clouds had to learn to listen very carefully.

Mrs. Cloudburst was careful to teach her little Clouds important lessons. One of the most important that the little Clouds learned from Mrs. Cloudburst when they went to the Rainbow Arches Nursery School in the sky was that everything in the sky and everything on the earth were connected. The little Clouds were to watch over the skies, and be guardians of all the people and all the little animals that lived on the earth below them.

Every day, before school ended, Mrs. Cloudburst gave one of her little Clouds in the class a special homework assignment. The little Cloud she picked would have to help some person, or animal on the way home from the Rainbow Arches Nursery School and then tell the class the following day all about how they were helpful.

Mrs. Cloudburst looked around her classroom just before the end of the school day today. Stripe the Cloud had been very good at following directions today. Mrs. Cloudburst said in her loudest voice, "Stripe the Cloud, I want you to help someone on your way home from school today and you can tell us about what you did tomorrow." Stripe the Cloud was very happy.

Stripe the Cloud could not wait until he got out of the Rainbow Arches Nursery School's gate. He was very excited about finding someone to help today. He looked down below him into Featherwood Forest. He saw Turnover the Turtle talking to his friend Patch the Cloud. Harriet the Hare was running around the forest trying to find someone to play with. Squiggles and Riggles the Squirrels were playing hide and seek in the tall trees. Today, all seemed well in Featherwood Forest.

On the top of the highest tree in Featherwood Forest, Witty the Owl looked into the distance. He had seen Lizzie the Lamb wander up the hillside. He thought that is was good for her to see other spaces and experience other places. He felt too, that it was important not to always take the easy path. But it is just as important to listen to others, and to be careful about the decisions that we make. Sometimes those choices make us better. At other times, the choices we make teach us very important lessons. Sometimes those choices make us wiser. Sometimes we need the help of others when we make bad choices.

Witty the Owl was glad that Lizzie the Lamb had learned some of those important lessons and that she had found her way home to her mother, after a very difficult journey. She knew she had made her mother sad and worried and would never do that again. Witty the Owl also knew that Lizzie the Lamb already had the courage to move beyond what was comfortable for her, and one day she would find her own field to call home. Up in the sky, Stripe the Cloud was a very happy Cloud indeed. He had been able to help Lizzie the Lamb when she needed it the most.